A FATE OF CROWNS NOVELLA

REBECCA L. GARCIA

RUIN

Editing by Angie Wade at Novel Nurse Editing
(www.novelnurseediting.com)
Cover Design and formatting by Dark Wish Designs
(www.darkwishdesigns.net)

DEDICATION

This novella is dedicated to my editor and friend, Angie Wade, who has made me into a better writer and never fails in her humor to give me a great experience while embarking on our red-penned adventures.

CHARACTER GLOSSARY

Evangeline: Princess of Berovia & sorceress

Caspian: Light fae

Zalia: Princess

The Necromancer

<u>Secondary characters:</u>

The King

Selena: Princess

Primrose: Princess

Crowley: Prince

Maverick: Prince

Charleston: Prince

CHAPTER ONE

My fingernails were caked with dried blood and mud. With the sword in my trembling hands, I tilted my head upward to watch as life left his pale-gray eyes. He was older today, fragile without the gold crown on top of his head. His conker-brown waves turned silver, then white. My lips curled up when he took his final breath. He was the last one I needed to kill, and now I had to die.

One Week Earlier

The west wing of the palace was too quiet for most, but I relished the absence of people. I ran my fingers over a well-creased spine, turning the pages of an ancient, leather-bound book until I found the spell. Pausing over the directions for my sacrifice, I smiled. It was simple enough. A small rodent would do.

Speckled crimson coated the round, frayed blue rug beneath my feet. I'd done my best to remove the stains, but there had been too many spillages of blood for soap and water to hide. They were a reminder of the monster I had become, with each passing day, every sacrifice, but they were justified; I'd been wronged too many times.

I caught my reflection in one of the two tall blue vases that stood on either side of the fireplace. I looked beastly, inside and out. Touching my cheek, I averted my gaze from my cracked exterior.

"It is time." I whispered to my master, who spoke to me through the magic that resided in my soul. His voice resonated inside my head.

"Make your sacrifice," he demanded, tugging at the ghastlier parts of my mind. Sunlight sprayed through a crack in the red drapes, illuminating the dust particles floating over the bookshelf. Lines of neatly packed books, filled with information on both kingdoms—Berovia, my home, and Magaelor, our rival—sat fading from the direct sunlight.

Breathing in a deep, anxious breath, I crossed my legs as I sat in front of the unlit fire. My gaze trickled up to the mantlepiece and the large mirror hanging above it. I inhaled sharply, then looked back at the text. After placing the grimoire on the floor, lying it open at the page of the ritual, I began preparations for the spell. My family would despise me more than they already did if they knew what I'd done. Their misfortunes were my doing, but it served them right for turning the other way while I had suffered. No one but my sister Zalia even acknowledged my existence, and she only did out of spite—a grudge long held against me for crimes that were not my own.

It didn't matter. I was working toward something much bigger. Until then, smaller spells would be enough to satisfy the revenge in my heart, causing them inconvenience and slight suffering that I took pleasure in watching. I had never been above bitterness. it's hard to be when I'd been forced to live in the shadows like a creature of the night, only allowed out to stroll the gardens when it suited my father. Oh, how he looked over us all, the immortal king who wore the three out of five objects of kai with pride, believing himself invincible. He did not age like the rest of us. In his seventies, he appeared thirty. The Ring of Immortalem gave him eternal life. He promised, to appease my siblings, that when he was ready to pass the crown to my sister—a throne that should have gone to me—he would live out the rest of his days on one of the islands off the coast of Berovian shores. I saw him for the liar he was, but my sister would not be as easily convinced.

The other two objects, the Sword of Impervius, which could kill any immortal, and the Amulet of Viribus, gave my father strength, agility, and speed that could outmatch any other. With them, he was feared, even by the fae who occupied the east of Berovia. Now that sorcerers finally had power over them, the king would do anything to keep it that way. Like most sorcerers, he hated them.

The bells from the tower rang loudly in the distance. I whipped my head around to look at the open window, in time to watch a flock of crows take off in flight like ink blots against the rising sun. Stone walls emerged from the shadows. I smiled as the orange kissed night into day.

The king would have left by now, as he always traveled at dawn. He would ride east to visit the light fae court under pretenses of peace. Sorcerers had never been kind to the fae, and my father was trying to change that, if only to meet his own wants of ruling the entirety of Berovia under false notions of equality. Even with the power to kill them, he wouldn't be granted their crown. He would have had to use his diplomacy to get his hands on their reign.

The fae were kind creatures. They looked like us, except for the wings that could fold against their backs, and ears pointing through their silky hair. I wondered how easily the fae king would enter the treaty if he knew what my father did with faeries who strayed into our half of the kingdom. My father locked them in the dungeons and strained them of their magic until they desiccated, becoming husks of what they once were, then they were hidden behind walls. I'd heard enough gossip to know. Tunnels behind the tapestries in my room led to different parts of the castle, rooms where words were spoken in secret. They were places I could go to and listen without being seen. They trapped the fae's powers inside the same relics and jewelry our people used to channel their powers—elemental magic, a practice I had long relinquished.

My strength came from the energy I harnessed from a strong, governing force. I had never met him, my master, but I spoke to him, and he looked after me as he did all who served in his magic. I remembered the day like it was yesterday. I was just a child, lost in tears and fear when he had come to me. He was but a voice in my head, one that talked me out of a depression threatening to take me. I'd lost everything, but he was there for me, whispering promises of justice and vengeance, of beauty and power, and when I turned seventeen four days ago, he vowed more. I was no longer a child but a woman, one who had the strength to do what was needed.

"I will help you take it all." He was good at that, assuring me of the desires of my heart.

"Master. Please accept this sacrifice. As always, I am in your debt." I exhaled slowly, looking at the ground. "With this spell, my sister's vanity

will become their undoing as it has been mine."
Father was gone, and I was only brave enough to
do my spells in his absence. I couldn't risk getting
caught, not when I was so close.

My master's sadistic laugh tinkled in my head.

Leaning forward, I grabbed an iron poker and
shuffled the logs until I found him, the rat I'd
spelled to sleep, then stored in the fireplace. It was
never lit. It was far too hot in Berovia for an
indoor fire, making it the perfect holding place. I
shuffled back and placed his furry body onto my
ritual plate, a large clay circle with symbols
engraved into it. I closed my eyes. The blackness
allowed me to focus, pinpointing the magic inside
my soul. I repeated the spell over and over, flexing
my fingers as I did. Cold crept through my veins
and stopped at the tip of my toes. A tightness
pulled at my chest, and my heart pounded. I
opened my eyes, then ran my dagger through the
creature. As I did, I pulled its pain into myself so
it would not suffer. Blood splattered on my arms

and over the ritual plate and moved like veins toward each symbol, creating a star.

My lips parted as his soul departed. A swirling ball of white, encompassing light that moved in on itself rose from the rat's body, then fizzled out.

"Do you feel the power in your veins, the strength I have bestowed upon you?"

I inhaled deeply. "I do."

"You can have more. You know what you must do."

I swallowed hard and licked my lips. "I can't do that. Not now."

"Then when?" he asked, and I felt his patience growing thinner.

"Soon."

I exhaled shakily. The ugly spots I'd cursed my sisters to wear would take time to break out through their skin. I guessed it would be in full bloom by tomorrow.

After wiping the blood from my arms and the few drops that had missed the plate and landed on the floor, I threw the stained cloth under my pillow. Then, I gathered the body left behind by the rat, stood, and walked over to the arched windows. Holding it by the tail, I dropped it out of the window, the fall bringing back memories I'd rather forget.

The sun glistened higher, warming blues to more oranges, radiating a golden hue over the land. The corners of my lips curled up. Mornings had never failed to take my breath away. The kingdom boasted of hot, unrelenting weather and humid days that gave illusion to wavering horizons, but the sunrises and sunsets were worth it.

Rolling my eyes downward to the freshly cut grass and trimmed bushes, I saw my brothers, Crowley and Maverick, waiting next to flowerbeds of reds and green. Horses were led to them by mucky, dirty-faced stable boys. Gold saddles shined from the stallion's backs. The young princes footed the stirrups of the black horses, then climbed onto their backs. They were going hunting, again. I envied their freedom. I lusted after their lifestyle, not just theirs but my sisters' too—Zalia, Selena, and Primrose. While I had the prettiest of their names, Evangeline, I did not inherit my parents' looks. I was my father's greatest shame, and after my mother's death, I was locked away for it. I was the princess who had morphed with age, from a beautiful baby with shining green eyes and bright blonde hair to a horrid thing.

I walked back toward my four-poster bed when I caught a glimpse of myself in the mirror. My eyes flitted from one disappointing feature to the next. My hair was thinning, and bald spots receded my hairline. Some of my teeth were missing, and a shadow of thin hairs sat over my thin lips. Angry, red spots covered my face, and scars and craters from popping them lay thick underneath. Heavy, tangled eyebrows weighed over my emerald-green eyes. I had talons for nails that I attempted to keep cut short, but no matter how hard I tried to correct my appearance, nothing changed.

My siblings were as beautiful as the next. It wasn't fair, yet they weren't really responsible for it. They weren't the ones who had locked me away, and in all honestly, I didn't know them very well. Perhaps I was making a mistake by punishing them. My father was the one responsible for keeping me up here. My gaze led to the grimoire. Had I gone too far?

Biting down on my tongue, I kept my scream behind tight lips. I wrapped my hands around my waist, doubling over as pain seared through me. "No, please." I dug my nails into my skin, creating half-crescent marks in my flesh. Time passed slowly, each second delving me into further agony. I choked on each breath, and my lungs growled. My hands and feet prickled. Every inch of me was raw with pain. "I won't stop." I spluttered through waves of torment, then it stopped. Just like that. Tears fell from the corners of my eyes. I let out a long, shaky exhale when it finally subsided. I pulled my knees to my chest and rocked back and forth.

My master saw my regret as defiance, as weakness, and there was nothing he hated more than fragility. Even my thoughts were not my own.

A loud knock resounded at my door. The smell of beef stew wafted into my room. I jumped to my feet and wiped the tears from my face. I grabbed the ritual plate and shoved it under a pillow, then kicked the book under the sofa. I glanced around one last time, looking for obvious signs of blood before clearing my throat. "Come in."

A servant with dirty-brown hair carried a silver platter.

"Over there." I pointed at the little table next to my bed.

She nodded, left the tray, and hurried out. None of the staff ever made eye contact. Their orders were simple: don't engage me in conversation. I'd gotten used to loneliness though, enough to enjoy my own company. On the instances I had been allowed to leave my room and walk the gardens, I would sneak to watch the nobles and ladies. That was when I had learned what a uniquely beautiful gift my father had unknowingly granted me; I liked myself. Most others distracted themselves with people, entertainment, music, food, and anything to prevent being alone. I wondered if they could see the truth, that the majority didn't like themselves. They weren't alone; I couldn't stand them either. Seldom had I come across a good heart or seen a single person who didn't come to life from gossip or kill over material things, but then, I'd only watched from the corners. Maybe up close, they could be different.

The stew smelled good, made with beef, gravy, potatoes, and herbs from the castle gardens. I noticed a few sliced carrots had been thrown in too. My stomach groaned in response. She'd bought me tea as well, honey and lemon, and four crackers on the side. It wasn't much. The bowl was small too.

I snapped my fingers, picturing what I wanted in my mind and letting it float on the edge of power. When I opened my eyes, the crackers had turned into slabs of chocolate. I grinned. Mastering sacrificial and ritualist magic took time, but I was getting better at it every day. I was tapping into unlimited power, and not all of it required a spell. I could perform the same things my people did when they used elemental magic by channeling with relics or jewelry. It was only when my powers were meant to harm when I had to take more brutal measures, such as offering a soul.

I eyed the fireplace where I placed sleeping creatures for my next enchantment. So much bloodshed, but such reward. In the moments I caught myself wanting to leave it all behind, I was reminded of one truth: not one person had shown me kindness in my miserable life, except my master. Girls like me needed to fight and make power for herself. Practice made perfect, and I needed a lot of it if I was going to have enough strength to take the throne from Father, force my siblings into submission, and earn love from my people.

"To achieve all you desire, you must acquire the darkest of magic," the voice whispered in my head, as it did every time my secret plot surfaced. *"You know what you need to do."*

I squeezed my eyelids shut. He'd been tempting me for far too long, and I grew closer to toppling over the edge with each passing day.

I touched my cheek lightly and brushed my fingertips against my cratered skin. The offer was as tantalizing as it was dangerous. It would mean forming a permanent shadow on my heart. After all, taking a human life was the worst thing one could do.

"Knock, knock."

Her voice made me jump. I jolted back, then kicked the book under the sofa again just in time. "Zalia." I hissed. "My least favorite sister." Her round, blue eyes searched mine as she stepped into the room. Her silky, black waves tumbled down her back, and her olive skin complimented her cherry-colored lips. She had inherited my grandfather's sharp features.

"What have you been doing?" She looked around us both. "I smell magic in the air."

"Eating dinner." I gestured toward the empty bowl. "You know I don't practice."

She rolled her eyes. "Oh, the lies." Zalia plopped herself onto the plush blue sofa, knocking a pillow onto the marble floor. I grabbed it before she could bend down to retrieve it herself, then propped it behind my back. I sat on the armchair opposite her, tapping my fingers rhythmically against the arm. I glanced downward and spotted the corner of the book sticking out.

Zalia fiddled with a necklace. I recognized the brilliant shade of purple, which sparkled when the light hit it. My gaze hardened. "That's mine. Mother gave it to me before she died."

"Was yours," she said, correcting me. "Father said I could have it, seeing, as you just pointed out, you have no use for it. What is the point in wearing a family relic if you're not going to channel magic through it?"

I wanted to slap the smirk off her face. *Tomorrow her face will be covered in puss-filled warts,* I thought, calming myself as I watched her cross her legs and look around.

"You know what? It looks good on you." A smile played on my lips. "You need something to distract from your awful personality."

"Oh, come now." She leaned forward. "Don't be jealous."

My face reddened. I grazed my fingers against the back of my neck. "What do you want?"

"Tell me what you're up to. I can sense darkness in here. The others may not believe me, but I know you're up to something."

My heart was pounding, but I didn't give anything away. "I don't know what you're talking about." I shrugged my shoulders, then tilted my head back. "My paranoid sister."

Her nostrils flared. "You don't deserve to call me that."

I scoffed. "You're unfair."

A stray lock of hair danced around her forehead, but she pushed it back. "The evil in you shadows this family. Whatever you're up to, I will find out." She pointed her finger at me. "We're not children anymore."

Memories flashed between us. She would follow me anywhere when we were little. I'd climb trees, and she was never far behind. She'd pick me the prettiest flowers from the meadows past the trees. We were inseparable until the *accident.*

"Careful, Zalia." My eyes bulged. "If you think me capable of such dark things, then I'd be cautious with empty threats."

She wrung her hands. "I wish Father could hear you. He'd have you beheaded for whatever it is you do up here." Her nose scrunched.

I looked over her head. "That would be difficult without evidence."

She huffed. "Did you know Logan came to court?" She glared, contempt in her eyes. "You were supposed to marry him, right? It was set up until Father decided to lock you away."

"You really are a vain little gnat."

She chuckled. "Oh my, it didn't take long for the insults to come hurling out. No matter, I greeted him." She ran her finger along her bottom lip. "He's such a good kisser, you know."

"Get out of my room!" I spat between my teeth. "If you've come here to gloat—"

"I have come here because I know you're the one doing bad things to our family." Her voice grew louder with each beat. "Strange things keep happening, and you're the only one in this castle horrid enough to do something like that."

"What exactly are you accusing me of?"

Her eyes flitted from me to my bed, then to the fireplace. "I don't know yet."

"If you have no proof and no idea, then I suggest you leave."

"Don't get too comfortable." She stood and crossed her arms over her chest.

"I never was," I called behind her.

She stormed out, puffing her cheeks as she left. Once the door closed, I dropped to my knees and grabbed the heavy, leather-bound book. With her on my tail, performing a spell was a bad idea, but it was too late to rebuke it now. Tomorrow they'd be ugly for a short while, and Zalia would know it was me. To my father's knowledge, I didn't practice. I dared not touch elemental magic. It was never my friend. But this power... it was from another place, and it didn't discriminate. Regardless, not a soul could know because Zalia was right about one thing. I would be executed for it, for heresy.

"You could make her pay," my master reminded me. *"She deserves it. They all do. After all, what is a heart? You could stop the pain for good."*

Orange rays peeked through the window, covering everything in its dewy glow. I fumbled my fingers, then closed my eyes.

"Take it from them before they take me from you."

I was jittery. I snapped my teeth together to stop the chattering. If Zalia found out and could prove what I was doing, I'd be dead, and if she didn't, it could take years to gain the power to fight them.

I sighed, and my voice grumbled in my throat. "Tell me what to do."

"It is time, Evangeline, to steal another's heart."

CHAPTER TWO

I'd prepared everything, including the dagger which had been welded with magic to remove the pain that came from a sharp blade. It was the little comfort I could offer my victims, which had, up until now, been small animals. For the power I needed, my master demanded a greater sacrifice.

My heart pounded as I walked the corridors. Candlelight flickered against the ancient, washed stone and portraits with eyes that looked like they were following me. Slinking into the shadows, I curved around the corner to where the ladies gathered after dark to gossip.

Their dresses billowed around them as they sat on the benches, and their hair was tied into knots on the back of their heads, each with two curls left to dangle around their faces. I could smell the honey and blueberry hues of their liquor from where I watched. They were drinking Abarini.

The chatter grew louder under the pale moonlight. There were twelve of them that I could see.

Ivy, strangling pink wildflowers and white daisies, was wrapped around the columns behind them, which led to the gardens. Guards were stationed at every entrance. A flash of silver penetrated the darkness where I stood when moonlight hit one of the guard's swords. I held my breath, then pushed back against the wall.

There she was, my beautiful target. She was tired of her bun and pulled her long, dark curls over one shoulder. Her dusty pink lips were forever turned into a smile, balling her bronzed cheeks. She danced, her pink ruffles twirling out around her, clearly intoxicated.

"She is perfect. With her death, you will be one step closer to the throne," he whispered, strengthening my resolve.

Watching her was exhilarating. She was everything I wasn't. Bright-eyed, she leaned forward talking over the others, excited for every passing moment. She lived in the present, reminding me of the second youngest, Selena.

Scraping two gold pieces across the bench toward the girl next to her, she laughed. "I always pay my dues. I lost the bet."

The other girl rolled her expressive blue eyes. "I knew Maverick wouldn't be interested. Seduction never got a girl anywhere with the prince."

Fuzziness swarmed my line of sight when light flickered to where I stood. I rolled my body away from the light of the flames, pushing myself behind a wall. They'd pointed a torch in my direction, the fire licking around the rag tied to the end of the wood.

"What is it, Dalia?" my target questioned.

"I thought I saw something."

"It's getting late. We've had our share of liquor for one night." She chuckled, shrugging it off. "Good night, ladies."

I pressed my finger against the dagger. I'd sharpened it especially for the occasion. When I heard her footsteps approaching, I squished myself between a gap out of sight. She rushed past, not noticing my presence.

Quiet as a mouse, I crept behind her, using slivers of darkness to camouflage myself. She danced her way through empty corridors, stumbling over her feet as she did. A spray of moonlight fell over the red carpet from a tall, arched window. The girl climbed up onto the edge, grabbing a handful of her skirts off the ground. Stars pinpricked the black, humid night. "Beautiful." She gasped, looking out over the home she had grown up in. Most of the girls had been brought here as children, then raised within the walls, taught etiquette, and made into ladies-in-waiting, to tend to the princesses' needs.

I was not bestowed such privilege. I wondered, bitterly, if my sister would cry for her lost friend.

I stepped forward, dagger pointed outward. Slices of white light illuminated my murderous eyes. I enjoyed the hunt more than I cared to admit. I'd attempted the moral high ground, the façade that I was above murder, but truth be told, I was the perfect monster. I had been carved by two decades of hatred, isolation, and pain.

Fear hesitated me when I reached her back. She didn't turn, too captivated with the world ahead of her. Would it be like slaughtering an animal for my sacrifices? It was so wildly intimate, watching something die. I craved the last moments, wishing I could stretch them out, but in the end, all hearts had to stop beating.

I inhaled sharply. Her perfume lingered around us. She rubbed the side of her neck, then stumbled. She grabbed the frame but toppled, her fingers slipping.

"No!" I grasped a handful of silk.

She screamed and pulled forward, almost dragging me with her. I pulled back with a burst of strength, and the side of the blade pushed against my stomach. We both fell, landing into a heap of dresses and limbs. Her scream had alerted all close to our presence. Footsteps carried through the corridors. She turned her head from the pile we were in and looked me in the eyes. She smelled like spring flowers. Her eyes were large with fright.

"You're the princess, aren't you? The one they hide?"

Her chest was heaving, and her hands shaking. I held the handle of the dagger tightly, until my knuckles turned white. There was no way I could kill her, cut out her heart, *and* make my escape in time.

I scrambled to my feet, then hightailed it out of there just in time for them to reach her. Sweat dripped down my forehead and into my eyes. I gulped in precious air as I reached my room. I ran my hands down the door, looking for the handle. I pushed it down and fell into the confines of the bedroom.

Relief pulled the weight from my shoulders. I hadn't killed anyone.

Yet.

But all I had done was delay the inevitable.

She had seen my face. No one knew I left my room at night. I could have let her fall to her death, and I should have. She mustn't have been allowed to see me and live to tell the tale. I prayed she would keep her seeing me to herself, but I knew her type; gossip was their livelihood, and I was the biggest rumor of them all.

Darkness squeezed the air from my lungs. Pain pricked my fingertips. I didn't sacrifice the girl, and now I would be punished.

***

Eyes paler than the moon watched me from the shadows. Lips bluer than glaciers grinned when I whimpered. Branches reached down like fingers, trying to grab me.

"Yours or theirs?" the man whispered, his voice echoing into a thousand shards around us.

I tried to escape by breaking into a run, but invisible constraints pulled me back, rooting me to the spot. He tilted his head and looked at me from the darkness of the forest. The tree line wasn't far, but how had I been so stupid as to enter the trees knowing what waited for me?

My heart hammered against my chest. A sheen of sweat coated my forehead. In the humid night buzzed thousands of insects, their songs erupting around us.

The forest was alive, and so was he. No longer a soul that echoed in my thoughts, he was flesh and bone with eyes redder than the flames of hell.

I snapped open my eyelids. My breaths rattled as I sat upright. Looking around my empty room, I sighed with relief. I was alone, but not for long. My master had penetrated my dreams, twisting them into nightmares and warning. I'd never promised him such sacrifice until now, but he was impatient. The keeper of ritualistic magic. The necromancer. The last of his kind. He wanted human hearts… hers.

Yours or theirs.

The words swung back into my mind.

I had to kill someone. Tonight.

CHAPTER THREE

I blew out a long, weary breath. Zalia's eyes were wild, her lips downturned. She looked positively murderous. Her hair was the same color as the trees that broke off into knotted branches in the woods to our left, so different to my blonde strands.

She pushed me against the stone wall, knocking the air from my lungs. Her heavy breaths hit my nose. "I know it was you!" she said accusingly behind clenched teeth. On her face were angry, red pimples with whiteheads threatening to burst at any moment.

I curled my lips behind my teeth, holding back my laughter. "You look awful," I managed to say, before letting a chuckle escape my lips.

She growled under her breath. "Father will not listen. He believes you wouldn't turn to dark magic, but I know." She loosened her grip on my shoulders, slumping me down the stone wall. "I know, and I swear I will reveal you for all you have done. The strange hexes and animal sacrifices... I told Father that the devil lives within these walls, but I didn't tell him it is *you*."

"It sounds like you have a lot of accusations." I glared, tensing my arms.

Her eyes rounded the way they had when she was a child, when curiosity took her and magic was beautiful. The glimpse of innocence softened my heart, carrying me back to days lost to time. "Why do you hate me so much?" My words were clipped by short-winded gasps as I attempted to catch my breath. "I was there for you when you were a child. I loved you."

The corner of her eye twitched, and her nose scrunched. "You know why."

"If you mean the accident—"

"Accident?" She scoffed. "We both know what *really* happened."

Finally, she'd said the words aloud. We both knew for years that she blamed me, but neither of us were willing to speak first, for the memory was too painful. "I never hurt him," I countered. "Why would I?"

"You did."

My stomach dipped. "He was our brother. I never hurt him. I loved him."

"You ruin anything that loves you. You are ruin. Our brother, sweet and young, he lies as bone and skull in a mausoleum, a life ahead never lived because of you." She pointed her finger into my chest.

Tears prickled in my eyes. "That's why you hate me so? You believe me a murderer?"

"I know what I saw."

"I was helping you!" I exclaimed, my eyes wide. "Your magic was out of control. I saved you."

Tears streamed down her face. "No," she cried, the blue in her irises scattering my shocked reflection. "Even if it were true, which it is not, then at what cost? You've grown darker with each day, hexing us, forcing us to suffer as you do. Our father despises you. We all do. Bless us all and leave this castle. You are nothing here."

I parted my lips, and tears pooled between them. I watched her walk away, my defence silenced in my throat. Despite years of hatred, she still had power over me. Promises made in childhood ran the deepest. Her honesty ached my soul; it slid down my neck and lay densely in my chest. She wanted me gone, believing I was somehow responsible for the demise of our youngest brother, Charleston. He was father's favorite. He had such big eyes—everyone who saw him commented on them—and a smile that filled me up. He was the sweetest of our brothers, although the king had seen a warrior in him. My father had envisioned strength, a ruler in Charleston, taken away only by his place in birth order. His death had ruined us all, but mostly the king.

The memory floated back to me. I tilted my chin, trailing my gaze over the stone washed by the sun and pausing at spikes reaching up into the light blue. My eyes snapped back to the ground when I recalled the sound of Charleston's skull crunching when he hit the path. I shuddered, despite the heat. A crack in the stone stared back at me. Crimson had soaked it for the rest of the day after he fell, and although it had been cleaned since, I swore I could still see a tint of red.

Zalia was wrong to accuse me. She had been twisted and warped by guilt and fear. She'd lost control, as she often had. She and Charleston had gone to the tower to play make-believe games, and her imagination had fallen too far from reality. When I found them, he was on the ledge of the window, begging Zalia to let him down. She didn't remember any of it, her mind blocked from the horrors of her past. I tried to grab him before he lost his footing, but I was too late. Perhaps it was why I had saved the girl in the window from falling, reenacting a time when I couldn't save him.

I rolled my eyes up to the sun. Spots filled my vision when I refocused on the gardens. Flowerbeds sprouted the most beautiful golden sanitas and purple wildflowers. The castle was quiet, and Father had allowed me to walk the gardens while the rest ate their midday feast. It was the only time I could leave my room. A butterfly landed on my wrist, fluttering its wings to a close. Mesmerized by the beauty of its royal blue wings and yellow markings in the center, I didn't notice him approach me.

He cleared his throat. "My lady, forgive my brazenness, but—"

"Oh my!" Jolting backward, I sent the butterfly into flight. I looked him up and down. His bright blue orbs lit up when he smiled, and his ears pointed through waves of golden hair. I thumbed my neck, and my face flooded with color. "I didn't know anyone else would be out here." I couldn't believe I was talking to one of them, a faery.

He shot me a dimpled smile. I averted my gaze, looking at the daisies peppering the ground.

"I needed to get away." He smirked. He was obviously a noble, even for a faery. "It's not often my kind is invited to court."

"I happen to like the fae."

"There is no need for flattery."

"It's the truth," I replied. "If the rumors are true, then you must be able to tell."

"Your honesty is refreshing. Some of your court forget that we can tell when they're lying."

"Hmm." I smiled. "I don't share their prejudices." Truth was, I had always admired the fae. They could whisk themselves up into the skies. They were kind, immortal, and beautiful. They cared not for money or crowns, but instead enjoyed every moment, playing games and engaging their senses. Even if they did allow their chaos to hold them back from greatness.

"I'm Evangeline." I offered my hand, which he kissed. I'd seen other highborn girls do the same, so I figured I'd copy.

"I am Caspian, the newly appointed ambassador." His eyes narrowed as he took in my dress, my tiara, and necklace. "Who are you? I mean, your title. A noble girl?"

I spluttered for words. He was a few inches taller than me and smelled like lavender and rain. His gaze was soft, but his eyebrows were pulled downward. I wasn't used to the attention from anyone, let alone someone like him.

"You're kind, but honestly, I'm no one."

"It's sad you believe that."

I shook my head. "It's complicated."

He held out his arm. I stared at it blankly.

"Save me the embarrassment and take it."

I ran hot all over. I wished he'd stop staring at me. Suddenly I was aware of every flaw on my face. He grinned. I wished he wouldn't.

"Accompany me. I'll get lost again. The castle is a maze."

My throat was scratchy, my palms sweaty. I shifted from foot to foot. My heart skipped a beat. My entire family walked into the gardens, guards not far behind. "I should go," I whispered, stepping backward.

Caspian looked from me to the royals. "Yes, I wouldn't want to anger them on their after-dinner walk."

I pressed my lips tightly. Zalia had joined them. I assumed she had encouraged their walk in the gardens as a way cut short my freedom. My bottom lip trembled, and my nostrils flared.

"Are you okay?"

I exhaled slowly. "Yes."

The guards wore the royal crest on their uniforms with pride. My father strode ahead of the others, with only a lady-in-waiting at his side. Another of his playthings, I presumed. The ruby on his silver ring glistened in the midday sun. I cast my eyes to my sisters. They were hiding their faces. The king must had forced them to continue their royal duties, no matter their spots on the verge of bursting open.

Puss oozed from one of Zalia's. I'd have felt bad if I weren't alone while they indulged in royal luxuries. I rolled my eyes when I spotted a dragon's eggshell hanging from Primrose's yellow dress. She was petite and pale, and she hurried behind Zalia. She covered her cheeks with her small hands. Her blonde waves danced behind her when she walked.

Caspian tutted. "How decadent. Dragons' eggs."

"It's vulgar," I said in agreement. "They keep them caged up, capturing them from Ember Mountains, with difficulty. A delicacy, one the royals partake of often."

His mouth twisted in disgust. "Tortured to provide them with lunch." He spat, his face growing paler by the second.

I narrowed my stare. "Yes, but what can we do?"

I watched Zalia walk, an umbrella held above her head by one of her ladies to shade her from the sun. Her broad shoulders and chiseled physique made her look more masculine than the other two. Still she was beautiful and the most cunning. The last was Selena. Her thick, luscious dark-brown curls were tied into a ponytail. Her almond-shaped green eyes looked steadily ahead. She was the only one not covering the red bumps and whiteheads. She walked proudly, her gaze cool and collected. She was slim but curvy in all the right places. She had olive-colored skin. She walked with such grace that it would envy a fae. Behind them, my two brothers walked, both with their heads held high. Crowley was the shorter of the two, and his golden-brown hair glistened in the sun. He held onto the hilt of his sword, sporting a white suit with gold fastenings. Maverick was taller, stronger… a hunter. His green eyes fixed ahead, he walked with purpose.

"I'm sure you want to get back to the feast," I offered the fae. "Instead of being out in the blistering heat with me."

He grinned, side-eyeing me. "I'm quite enjoying the company."

My heart thudded, and my hands were clammy. Surely he didn't mean it. He couldn't be flirting with me. There were far better options, even for a fae at court. Anyone but me.

I looked at my father, who smiled widely until his eyes landed on me. A steel stare pushed adrenaline through my veins.

"It's time for me to disappear. Sorry," I whispered, then turned and ran.

"Wait, won't you…"

I didn't catch his question as I rushed to put distance between me and my family. Seeing my sisters embarrassed had only given me seconds of satisfaction. The spell would wear off soon, and they'd be back to being adored. I reached the secret passageway and sighed with relief. Ducking under spikes that pointed down in warning, I climbed into it, then emerged on the other side.

Cold, narrow passageways and ancient stone steps greeted me as I made my way up toward my room, far away from the rest of my family's chambers. The sun was gone and the shutters closed, and I was back to being alone.

"You should have killed when you had the chance. You promised a life and have not delivered." The voice resonated in my head.

My heart fluttered. I pushed open my bedroom door and screamed.

Seven dead crows laid in a circle on the floor. Blood markings surrounded them. The smell was overpowering.

"Now you will pay."

CHAPTER FOUR

Strangled screams sounded from behind jail doors. The stretching table sat stark under the candlelight and had been whittled to be used on faeries' wings. The room dropped several degrees. I shouldn't have ventured into the dungeons, but I had to find a human heart and fast, and who was better than a thief or murderer?

I'd cleared the birds from the floor last night and took their bodies to the woods when night had fallen. I was sick to my stomach. The necromancer haunted my nightmares. I did not get a single moment of peace, awake or asleep. When I awoke, I knew I needed to end the torment.

I pushed on ahead, looking for my victim. The only innocents in the dungeon were the fae. The rest were sorcerers, awaiting trial for their crimes. Shimmering caught my eye, pulling me to my right. A bucket of rubies glistened under the shuttered light pouring through the barred windows. They were untouched, yet to be filled with the magic siphoned from tortured creatures. Storing magic in relics and precious gems was smart, as it was the only thing, aside from gold and silver, that couldn't be replicated using magic. If only it weren't so barbaric. Rumors could be dismissed, but when it was in front of my eyes, the destruction was harder to ignore. I pondered how many rubies one fae could fill before it desiccated, pushed to the brink of death but never offered the sweet release.

"These souls are too broken," the voice warned as I approached locked doors. *"I need vibrance, vitality, youth…"*

I ran my hands down my face, pulling the skin under my eyes. There was no way I could find that girl from the other night without being seen or kill her without arousing Zalia's growing suspicion.

"I don't want this." I choked. "I'm not a murderer."

"You could have everything. Be a queen."

The words fell like poison from his cold, blue lips. He gripped my soul, unveiling my wants and desires. I didn't know where his physical self was, but his location was of little importance. His reach was far, his hold suffocating.

Lifting my skirts from the ground, I ran out of the dungeons, leaving the tortured pleas and howling to the darkness under the castle. I emerged to a bustling corridor, ensuring I took the back passages people seldom roamed. I knew my way through the web of hallways better than any other.

"You again."

I jumped, my shoulders tensing on seeing Caspian again. His eyes flitted from mine to my dress. I knew what he must have been thinking;

my dress was far too beautiful for such an ugly maiden.

I shivered, then tilted my head to look around him. "I was actually about to—"

"Please. You left so quickly before."

His eyes were like sapphires, brighter than any I had seen. He was so captivating, his essence beautiful and alluring, a rose among thorns.

"I stay out of the way of people."

His eyes narrowed. "What do you mean?"

"It's not important."

"Then perhaps you can direct me to the dungeons."

My heart pounded in my chest. "Why do you want to visit there? It is the place for criminals."

He rubbed his forehead. "I can't say."

"You don't want to go down there."

He lifted an eyebrow, then whispered. "Why?"

I swallowed hard. "Things you will not want to see."

His gaze narrowed, his lips thinning into a hard line. "Exactly."

I gulped. If he found out what they were doing to his people down there, it could evoke a war. Immortals against sorcerers, in time the fae would win, as my father was one man and could not take on their numbers.

The only reason sorcerers were the reigning leaders was our ability to organize ourselves. Regrettably, I'd believed the fae were lesser than us when I was a child, until I was old enough I could make up my own mind. I'd read enough books and had listened in on more than one conversation to know enough about politics. We were taking advantage of them and always would.

"Are you cold?" he questioned.

His voice pulled me from deep thought. I blinked twice. "You were wondering if I'm cold?"

He laughed, the most beautiful sound. "Why is that such a surprise? You're shaking."

"Oh." I fumbled my fingers, then pressed my hands together. I was cold, but I couldn't admit it without arousing suspicion. It was warm in the castle, but my master was sucking the life out of me, as punishment, until I delivered him a human soul. "I'm fine, but thank you. Sometimes I shake for no reason." I guffawed, then fell silent. I had no decorum. "I apologize for my outburst. It's not often people show me kindness."

"It's their loss." He buried his hands into his deep pockets. He was dressed eccentrically, even for my taste, but then the fae always did wear things made from nature. His shirt looked as if it were woven from leaves, each of them shimmering with gold faery dust.

I could feel my cheeks burning with heat. I cursed internally at my body's obvious reaction, praying he wouldn't notice. A boy like him would be offended if his act of goodwill was taken the wrong way by someone like me.

"I don't understand why you do."

"Because you're beautiful."

I flinched. "Are you teasing me?"

"Why wouldn't I show you kindness? Besides, I cannot lie." He smirked. "Unless… Are you one of those criminals you talked of?"

I knew he was joking, but it held an uncomfortable truth. Had I not set out to murder another?

"Then you must be blind." I sighed softly and turned on my heel. I wouldn't be preyed on or humored.

"Wait!" he called, but I didn't look back.

He was obviously searching for something and using me to get it. Everyone had motive, but I knew it better to not look back. As much as I wanted to believe it, I couldn't help but see there was something innately good about him. For that reason alone, I needed to leave. I was where pretty things died. Speaking of beautiful things… I saw my sister turn a corner in the distance.

I hurried away down a desolated passage, my feet thumping against the ground as I did. Turning the corner, I ran cold. Blood dripped out of the cracks in the stone, trickling down into a pool on the floor. My hand shot up to cover my mouth.

"If you do not take a life, it will be your blood on the wall."

I blinked, and the blood disappeared.

"You."

I jolted on seeing her. She was one of my sisters' ladies. I recognized her jewelry. Although, I had to wonder what she was doing in this part of the castle.

The lady's voice was high-pitched and grating. "Wandering around alone?"

"I would ask who you are," I said, clearing my throat, "but as you're walking the back passages, you must be meeting a man. You're one of the ones sent to seduce men to find out what they're hiding for Zalia, aren't you?" I accused her, knowing my sister's reach throughout the castle and how she claimed so many secrets.

"What do you know of Zalia, and how does she know you?" Her viper-red eyes latched onto mine.

"I know lots of things. Now, get out of my way."

"You must matter for some reason. Zalia sent me to look for a misplaced girl." She twirled a lock of hair around her index finger. "A woman with a crown on her head and bitterness on her face." She looked me up and down. "I see I have hit my mark."

Unable to mask my scowl, I let out a long breath. "Zalia has always been resourceful, picking the saddest grapes in the bunch to do her bidding."

Her eyes narrowed. "You seem to know her well."

"Well enough. Regardless, you have failed her in your attempts to tail me. You let me know who you are. Stupid girl." I shook my head.

She took a step forward. "You wear a tiara."

"Yes."

She tapped her nail against her chin. "Ah, then you are the princess. The one hidden away," she proclaimed. "You were just a rumor at most. There are few who have claimed to see you, but no one truly knew. I thought Cara was mad when she told me you saved her from a fall."

I clenched my jaw. I should have let her fall. "Get out of my way."

She stretched out her arm, blocking my way out. "How intriguing, to be locked away by your own father. What crime did you commit? No?" she asked, as I refused to answer since it was obvious.

Could she not see? I was clearly hidden for my ugliness!

"No matter then. Zalia wanted you to know she's watching you." Her lip tugged at the corner. "Every step. I'm not the only one. There are many of us. Watch your back."

"Tell my sister that I think it is pathetic," I spat, "that she sent one of her puppets to send me a message."

I turned on my heel and marched away. Fury coursed through my veins, and my teeth almost shattered from the grinding. Zalia was walking a dangerous line, one that would end in one of our deaths.

CHAPTER FIVE

I sat the plate, with ritual symbols carved into clay, on the ground. The book lay open on a spell, but my master would not grant me the power for even a tiny spell unless I did his bidding first.

"Kill them, or I'll kill you. I will not ask again."

His hold on me grew tighter by the day, strangling my soul. It was an itch too deep to scratch, an ache too strong to ease. I closed my eyes, exhaling slowly.

"Please, don't," I whispered aloud.

"I will bequeath great power unto you. I will give you everything you desire. Beauty. Strength. Vengeance. All you must do is take one life."

I swallowed hard, pulling my fingers up to my throat and gently caressing the skin. "One life and no more," I said, relenting. "Just one." I ran through a list in my head. I could have taken one of my sisters' lives, releasing me from my vengeance, but I couldn't bring myself to hurt my family, no matter how estranged I was. Perhaps Zalia's lady who had followed me... She would have deserved it, but then Zalia would have suspected me.

The smooth walls around me felt like they were closing in, and the strings of my corset too tight. The silver, ornate framed mirror reflected over my room, above the unlit fireplace. Walking lightly over smooth stone floor, I approached my reflection with a solemn stare. Touching my cheek, I pondered what life must've been like for the beautiful. I could've had it all. To be in the highest of service to my people, a servant to the kingdom—a queen. My tiara could have been traded for the crown that sat upon my father's young curls, youth bestowed to him with a ring that granted him the immortality of a fae. No one could take it from him unless he chose to relinquish.

Unless *I* could.

With my master's power. There was no more evading. It was time.

I grabbed my traveling cloak, red with white trim. I pulled the hood over my face, then turned to the secret passageway that led out of my room and past the guards. They linked the old part of the castle with the newer rooms, but over time, they'd become a maze only I knew.

"It is time then," I said to myself, pulling strength into my trembling bones. "To kill."

***

There she was. The girl who had lived. She couldn't be allowed to leave. My master had already declared it so; she would die, and I would be the one to tear out her heart. He was growing impatient. He needed a young soul. I didn't know what for, but I knew better than to ask questions.

She sat surrounded by friends on a window ledge. Had she not learned her lesson? She threw her head back laughing at a joke I couldn't make out. In the daylight, I could see her better. She wore imperfections that made her look more human than flawless, like freckles smattered around her button nose and dark creases under the eyes that she'd done her best to conceal with white powder.

"Spying on girls you'll never have as friends? It's creepy."

I whipped my head around to look at Zalia. She pointed at the pimples covering her otherwise flawless skin. "They're still there." She growled under her breath. "When will your curse wear off?"

I tilted my head to the side, smirking. "Oh, that is unfortunate. Although, I think it is quite the improvement… Perhaps they will stay for good."

"That better not be true!"

"Evangeline." Caspian ran toward us, his breaths quickening.

Wide-eyed, I looked from Zalia to him. "I've found you…" He paused when he saw Zalia. "Your highness." He bowed. "Pardon the intrusion."

"I am amid a conversation with my sister."

He squinted under the light. "Sister? Wait, you're a princess?"

Zalia rolled her eyes. "How do you know one another?"

I looked at Zalia. "I bumped into him in the gardens. That was all."

"Well…" Zalia exhaled wearily. "Stay back in your room. If I found out you've left again for another midnight stroll, Father will rain his wrath down upon you." She snapped her fingers at Caspian. "As you are a guest to the court, faery, you may leave us."

He burned red, balling his fists at his sides.

"You must take my advice and stay away from this one," she stated. "She is nothing but trouble."

He unclenched his fists, then grinned, making me smile too. "I happen to like trouble, princess." He spat the word like venom. He was growing on me.

Her eyebrows wrinkled. "Disgusting." She shook her head, then pushed us apart. "I will have your chambers checked in an hour," she warned as she walked away.

Once she was out of earshot, I let out a sigh of relief. "Thank you."

"Princess."

"Yes." I flushed red.

"You left that out."

"I'm not an important royal. I was locked away."

"Why?"

I looked at him incredulously. "Look at me. I'm hideous."

Confusion swept his features. "Evangeline, you are the most beautiful woman at this court. I couldn't believe my luck when I spotted you alone, then you seemed to shy. It was surprising."

"You must be joking. I'm a beast." I ran my fingers over the bumps in my skin. "Every time I look in the mirror, I want to cry."

His eyes widened, then he tapped his finger against his chin. "Have you always been, um, forgive me for using your words, hideous?"

I inhaled sharply. "No."

"It just happened one day?"

I nodded.

"Ah. That makes sense."

"What?" I asked.

He shot me an amused look. "I don't see the ugliness you persist is there."

"Don't be kind."

"Really. You're beautiful."

He paused, spending far too long staring at me. I looked away, feeling naked and vulnerable. I wished he would stop staring. "You must be cursed." His tone was steady. Not a single shred of humor laced his words. He was being serious.

"I'm sorry?"

"Us faeries can see through curses and glamours. It's the only explanation I can think of as to why you do not see what I do. I see the real you, Evangeline, and regardless of the curse, it really isn't about how one looks when I choose who I befriend. Although, I admit it is why I first approached you." He placed his hand on mine, sending shockwaves through me. "I am immortal. Looks fade in time, but loyalty, strong spirit, and intelligence last a lifetime. Don't let anyone make you feel less than what you are, and more than that, don't let yourself believe it. You have such spirit. You do not see us as lesser than you. You were disgusted seeing the dragons' eggs. You have more kindness in your little finger than most have in their entire bodies."

My shoulders slumped. How I wished it were true. "You don't know me."

"I see you, Evangeline."

Tears fell thick and fast before I could catch myself. "I'm sorry. This is the first time..." I trailed off.

"You're overwhelmed. It's okay. You are okay."

His words grounded me. I felt the dagger inside my robe, and it weighed heavier than ever. I swallowed hard, attempting to remove the lump in my throat. "I must leave for my chambers."

"Wait." He grabbed my arm, lightly. His touch felt like stars. "I need your help." His eyebrows drew together, wrinkling his forehead. The light from the moon shone onto his face, paling his features. I could hear the ladies in the background, around the corner from us, too busy in their rowdiness to hear our conversation. "Can I trust you, Evangeline?"

I knew I could not lie to a faery. "You can trust me not to go to my father about what you say."

He smiled. "Ah, you'd do well at our court, you know. Dancing around the truth."

"What is it you need?" I questioned.

"My people are in the dungeons, being tortured."

I shuddered. It was what I had feared. "How did you get past the guards?"

He tapped his pocket, and the sound of coins clashing together told me he had bribed them.

"Disloyalty," I grumbled.

"They are tormenting them."

"I know." I hesitated, fumbling my fingers. "Who sent you here?"

"The king, or should I say your father, believes me to be the ambassador to aid in negotiations after his treaty with my people, but my king sent me to find out the truth. There were rumors about the sorcerer's treatment of our people, and now it is confirmed. I must free them, then flee."

"You've risked a lot by telling me this."

He grabbed his hands in mine and squeezed slightly. "I have learned, over time, who to confide in and not. I do not understand why, but I feel a pull toward you." He reached up and brushed his hand down my cheek, then my neck.

"You are a princess, but one so carelessly thrown away. Help me take revenge against those who would suppress not only me, not just my people, but you too."

"You saw a kindred spirit," I said slowly, uncertain in his trust.

"I tend to look for these traits."

I looked down at my feet. It was growing colder, not for anyone else, just me. My master was at the end of his patience, freezing me from the inside, forcing my hand until I took another's life. I needed to get away and kill before I was the one murdered. "No," I said, hoping it was enough to excuse myself, that he would let me leave. "Understand I will not tell my father, but I cannot aid you. My loyalty is to Berovia."

He let go of his grip on me and stepped back. "What has Berovia ever done for you?"

CHAPTER SIX

Lingering smoke from the fires was complemented by strong spices and charcoal. I'd never been to the kitchens before tonight. I peeled my eyes away from the doorway, which led out into the black of night, and turned my focus to the girl who lay dead at my feet.

I couldn't hear anything besides the insects in the gardens. I turned her head to the side with the sole of my shoe and pressed my lips together when I saw the poppy-colored bruise from when I'd hit her on the side of her head with a rock. It hadn't gone as smoothly as I'd planned. I could still hear her pleas from the last seconds of her life before I cut her throat.

She'd fought me when I'd come up behind her. The servant girl had been preparing pastries for breakfast. Some nobles had awakened early and demanded their food no matter the hour. She tried to stab me, but that's when I grabbed the stone. I'd thought the blunt trauma to the head would stop her, but she was a fighter until the very end.

Regret seeped into the corners of my cold heart, then I reminded myself why I had chosen this woman. Unlike us, the lowborn were not permitted to use magic, by the king's law. They labored with their hands and by the sweat of their brow. It was a difficult life for a servant, even one who served in the castle, but it did not excuse her actions. She climbed the ranks by any means necessary. She was cruel to children, and she was rumored to have poisoned a man, but then, I'd always found rumors to be revealing. She had a darkness in her that mine recognized, and I had chosen her. If I had to take a life, it wouldn't be an innocent's.

"You wanted youth," I said, hoping she would be enough. "She is no older than nineteen." I swallowed hard, feeling the weight of what I had done in my stomach. Blood was splattered over the uneven ground. Crumbs and flour had mixed with the blood, and I hoped it would pass as a wine stain once I scrubbed the ground. Crimson veined out over stone and pieces of hay, reaching my feet. First, I'd need to dispose of the body, and the moat was the best place I could think of. It was not too far to drag a body without being seen but was deep enough she wouldn't surface straight away.

"Finally, Evangeline, you are strong. One of mine."

Relief squashed my residual guilt. What I desired was in reach, power unmatched by any mortal.

The servant's soul twinkled out from her chest, rising in a glorious ball of light. I ran my hands down my face, sweat beading on my forehead.

The light was enraptured by darkness, swallowed whole.

I felt it before I heard him again. Power reached through me. It was strong, coiling around my center until I couldn't breathe. My broken body could not contain it. I'd made a mistake. My lips trembled, my hands shook, and my legs weakened. I fell to my knees, my hands seeping through the blood. Then, a headache came with stars that filled my vision. I squeezed my eyes shut in response. Pain ripped with each breath, any movement crippling me.

It felt like every cell in my body was alight with fire. I couldn't move and was certain I was about to die. What would become of me? A murderer. The afterlife did not accept such monsters. I'd be banished to the place of nothing, where souls ambled for an eternity, looking for shreds of their old lives, finding no happiness, stuck between worlds.

"NO!" I screamed, because I didn't want to die. Tears trickled down my face, patterning my cheeks with trails left behind.

"It is done."

The torment slowed, pulling me into a slumber I did not want but couldn't deny. I needed to move the body before anyone found us. It was almost six. Servants would be down soon. Before I could protest, my eyes shut, and I was in another place.

Shock erased all feeling. It was dark inside the lair of the beast. He snarled and grappled for the scraps of my humanity that were slipping away. I could sense every part of him, even the most vulnerable. If he gave into his humanity, then a thousand years of guilt and torment, beyond the realm any sorcerer or fae could comprehend, would descend upon him.

He howled into the night, and snakes hissed at the sound. Small animals thumped to the beat of his aching heart.

I cleared my throat. "Master." I had expected a strong figure, not this. "What is wrong?"

He stood straight, then tilted his chin, forcing away all agony in my presence.

"Now that you have your power, we can meet face-to-face." His voice echoed around us, bouncing off stone and jagged edges of gray. He emerged from the shadows. His eyes locked onto mine, sending shivers through my soul.

"I must awaken. Where am I?"

"You are asleep. Your body is in the kitchens, but your soul is here—for a time. Few have done what you have. Most are unwilling to sacrifice, but you are not weak like them."

I narrowed my eyes. Something didn't feel right. "You're hurting," I stated, my voice trembling. "I can sense it in every rattling breath. What is it that scares a necromancer who does not even fear death?"

He spat on the ground, and ink-black spots smattered the grainy floor. "Those who fear death fear freedom. Death is a release. It is peace. You young ones, so fickle." He ran one of his long talons over drawings on the stone wall. "Immortality is a curse, a life without anyone to share it with."

I could hear a woman's voice catching in the breeze, whispers that dissolved as quickly as they had come. "What is this place?"

"My home."

I swallowed hard. "That's it? You said a life without anyone to share it with… You must mean love. The voice, is that her, the person you wanted to share your life with?"

"You are observant."

"That's what happens when one is forced to live in the shadows."

He squinted. "A fate I understand all too well."

"What happened?" I asked. "We share power. I have proven myself to you. Please, tell me."

He inhaled deeply, then blew out a lonely breath. "She suffers a fate worse than death."

"What could be worse?"

"Her soul is shattered." His words were hollowed, as if he had repeated them thousands of times. "Pieces of it remain like dust particles, lost in all corners of this world. I can tap into parts of her, but only for a moment before she fades away."

"That's what you use your power for? To get a glimpse of her?"

"I cannot die because I will not leave her alone, without peace."

The hairs on the back of my arms stood erect, and tears pricked my eyes. It was the most tragic love story I'd ever heard. While he was a monster, I felt compassion for the man hidden behind layers of evil, created only to protect his heart and savor his love. "I'm sure she would have wanted you to be happy."

His expression faltered for a micro-second. I would have missed it had I not been staring at his blue, thin lips. We stood in silence with dripping from somewhere behind us as the only sound.

Lost in thought, I looked up at the crystals that shone from their homes among the crevices and holes. Gem blue and emerald green sparkled even in the dimmest light.

"I grant you great power," he said facing the wall, so I couldn't make out his face. "Go back to your body and show no mercy to those who hurt you, but take care." He paused, then turned to look back at me. There was an invasiveness to his stare that I wished to escape. "You are cursed. I sense it attached to every cell in your body. It stole your beauty from you at a young age."

My lips parted. I ran my fingertips along my skin, feeling the craters beneath my touch. "I was told, yes, but why am I cursed? How did this happen?" Looking down at my talons for nails, I sighed. Someone was responsible. As a baby, I was adored—beautiful, so I was told—then around the age of three, I changed. It wouldn't have pained me if it hadn't pushed everyone away from me and lost me my crown. "Tell me what I need to do!"

He flexed his fingers, forcing me to my knees with nothing more than a look. Agony ripped through me and tugged at my nerves, dropping me to the ground. I opened my mouth to scream, but no one could hear me there.

"Do not mistake my bringing you here and giving you power for vulnerability. I gave you magic, and I can take it away."

He clicked his fingers, and I breathed relief. I forced myself to my feet and looked at the monster once more. "I will not forsake you."

"You will remember your promise, for I am not known for being forgiving."

"Thank you," I whispered, then gathered my skirts, lifting them off the ground, and high-tailed it out toward the sheltered sunlight. As I did, I awoke to the sound of chatter growing outside of the room. I was too late to move the body. Before anyone entered, I ran through a connecting door, through another kitchen, almost tripping over a box, and out another door until I reached the edge of the gardens. My legs ached, and the skin on my hands were cracked. Blood stained my dress. I had to get back to my room, unnoticed, but how?

The castle had come to life with the rising sun, and guards were stationed at every entrance. I felt my newfound magic prickle in my fingertips. I closed my eyes, and the flowers around me wilted, then died. It moved through me like natural magic did in the fae, except mine was wicked.

It was unlike the Berovian's who channeled the elements, or the sorcerers in Magaelor who used ancestral magic, channeling it through their staffs and soil. Ritualistic and sacrificial magic was the only one with no bounds, but unlike natural magic, I could harm another with it. I was unbound by the laws of magic held by both kingdoms and the islands between.

Even the fae who live on both islands couldn't match my power. I raised my head, feeling more powerful than ever. I glanced in the direction of the trees. I needed a distraction. I closed my eyes, then willed it. Fire erupted, its flames licking their way over dry bark and dead leaves.

"Over there!" one guard called, followed by tens more. It only bought me minutes. As they ran in one direction, stomping over dead wildflowers, I ran in the other, toward the castle. When I reached it, I moved out of the way as a small crowd swelled steadily. Moving to the left, I reached the space under the castle leading to a secret passageway. After forcing it open, I crept down the stone steps that connected to one of the corridors in the east wing.

It was time to take back all that had been stolen from me. It was time for my reign.

CHAPTER SEVEN

I slammed my fist against his door, thudding four times before he answered. He pulled the door open, and I slumped down the wall. My eyes were heavy, bloodshot, and tearing up from the arrowed sunlight through a small window. This part of the castle was nicer than the west wing. It was close to the front, still far away from the rest of the royal family, and kept for visitors. Caspian would have been one of the first fae guests who hadn't been dragged to be tortured.

"You look like hell!" Caspian exclaimed, his eyes wild. When he extended his hand, I gripped it and he pulled me to my feet.

"Yes," I admitted. I'd only had a chance to change and hide the blood-stained dress before heading out. Not that it mattered, I always looked like hell, as he'd so eloquently put it.

"Have you changed your mind?" He tugged at the collar of his white shirt and looked me up and down. "Love?"

"Yes."

A slow smile spread across his face. "I am so happy to hear it."

"Wait."

His eyes widened. "Yes?"

"Please understand that although I agree to help you, I cannot let you take Berovia from us or start a war." I looked around the emptying corridor. "But I can do more. Please." I gestured behind him. "Invite me in."

He moved out of my way. "Please, Princess, come in."

His pants had been thrown on in haste. They were unbuttoned and wrinkled. Averting my eyes,

I looked around as he closed the wooden door. A rug stretched out to the corners of the room, which was much smaller than mine. A window, reaching from the ceiling to the floor, looked out to the gardens. A dressing table, white, marked and scratched, sat across from his bed. A mirror hung above the table, reminding me of why I had come.

"You were right. I am cursed."

He grinned. "I knew it."

"Careful." My expression darkened. "That smile could cost me a nation."

"Was that flirtation?" He feigned shock. "I didn't know you to be capable of such a thing."

I exhaled slowly. "Neither did I."

He sat on the end of his bed. "You're a natural."

I held my hands behind my back, fumbling my fingers. "The curse was confirmed."

"By whom?"

"No one important. All that matters is I'd been made to look like a beast to the world, and until you, I had no idea." I inhaled sharply. "Every time

I've seen my reflection, I've hated myself. I am the embodiment of a monster."

"Oh, Evangeline."

"Don't pity me."

"But I want to." He had kind eyes, the type that made a small part of me want to let him.

"Tell me. How do I remove it? You're a faery. You must know."

He looked up at a gold lamp that hung between two pictures, one of boats on the sea by the castle, the other a wood, with knights riding through the trees. I wondered where his mind had gone as he stared away blankly. "A curse can only be undone by the one who cast it," he explained. "To rid you of it, we first must find who placed it on you."

I tapped my finger against my chin. "The only ones I can think of who would do such a horrid thing to me are my family, my father in particular. He hates me."

"No man can hate his own child *that* much."

I swallowed hard. "You have *met* my father, correct?"

He chuckled. "I see your point, but, wait." He stood, then pulled out a chair for me to sit on.

I took my seat and he took my hand in his. Kneeling in front of me, our gazes locked, and I'd never felt so vulnerable.

"I'm sorry, Evangeline, that you have had such a lonely life and have been betrayed by your own blood. Nobody deserves what you have had done to you."

I touched the side of my neck. "I deserve it."

"I do not believe it."

He had such light in his eyes, and he had been the first to see it in me. I couldn't tell him the truth; I was a murderer. I may not have been ugly on the outside as was perceived, but on the inside, I was the wretched thing I'd been cursed to be.

"Help me," he said, breaking me from my dark thoughts. "If not to start a war, then to release my people from the dungeons. Take the Sword of

Impervius from your father. You know it is the right thing to do."

"The only weapon that can kill a fae," I stated.

He shook his head, then stood. "Not the only thing, but one of two. There is a dagger that exists too, but it is under our protection." He paced in a circle, holding his hands behind his back. "Kai created the five objects to being balance to the world. Immortality cannot truly exist. It is against nature. When we were created, so were the weapons that could end our lives." He looked down at his hands and the rings that shone from his fingers. "It is a mercy. No one should be made to live forever."

"He has three of the five. There have been whispers that he has been searching for the other two. Don't you understand what will happen if he finds them? He will become invincible." Caspian looked manic, even with the shadow over his face. His back faced the window, the sunlight surrounding him like a bright aura. "He is an unjust man—cruel, as it shows by what he did to you, his own daughter. He will hunt us. Bring the fae to our knees."

I pressed my hands together, then rested my chin on the tips of my fingers and let out a long, weary breath. "I am not an advocate for how the king rules. In fact, I oppose his means. However, I cannot condone your people's weakness. One sword can't slay you all. With a little organization, you could fight back. You have the numbers and the ability to heal yourselves, and you can't die. Don't you realize the army you hold? The numbers we have, the vast armies, are nothing but a delusion. We are mortal."

His lips parted, then his jaw slacked. He stared over the top of my head for a good minute before blinking. "You're right."

A part of me wished I hadn't enlightened him. I could have started a revolution, although their fatal flaw wouldn't allow it. They were the definition of chaos. Starting a war wasn't in their blood nor was violence.

"We do not wish to engage in battle unless absolutely necessary," Caspian said quickly, solidifying my thoughts. "You do, however, hold truth. All we wish to do is keep our land and take our people back from where they have been mercilessly held."

"How did you know?"

"You think my king does not have spies here at court? Not all sorcerers hate us."

I curled my lips together, behind my teeth. "I will help you get them away and remove the sword from my father's possession." I held a finger up, pausing him. "But I will not hand it over to your king. I will keep it, lock it away…"

He stopped pacing and sighed relief. "I am in your debt, Evangeline."

"Can you do something for me, in return?" I asked, itching the back of my neck.

"Anything for you, love."

His words sent tingles down my spine. I couldn't help but smile. "Tell me what I look like. I've not seen myself without the curse."

"Oh." His cheeks reddened.

"Did I embarrass a faery? Surely, it's not possible."

He gestured me to the bed and sat beside me. Looking deeply into my eyes, he blew out a long breath and pulled his lips into a smile. I wanted to touch the golden strands that looked like silk on his head, but I restrained myself.

"Why do you wear a tiara now but did not in the gardens when we met?"

"Oh. I don't wear it when I think I could be seen by the king. It would just anger him."

"Yet they let you keep one."

"Discreetly. I think it's just to keep me quiet. Appease me."

He puffed his cheeks out and ran his hand through his hair. "When this is done, you can wear your tiara all day long and in front of anyone."

I laughed, then flushed red. "*Please*. Would you?"

"Yes." He regarded me carefully, pausing on each feature. "Your eyes." His gaze softened. "They remind me of winter. The middles are the color of evergreens from our region, and the circle of black inside them embody the early night that comes with the season. Surrounding them is the most vibrant white, like freshly fallen snow. I feel like I am looking out upon frosty forests and tall mountains from my travels to the north of Magaelor. I could lose myself in them." His eyes flitted back and forth from each iris. "Beautiful and framed with midnight-black lashes."

My heart skipped a beat. "I was going to say yours reminded me of the sea." I let out a tense breath. "Now I fear I must go write a poem or sonnet about them as I cannot do justice to what you said about mine."

He laughed, and the sound tinkered around us. "We are known for our words."

"What about my skin?" I asked, picturing the abrasions, puss-filled spots, warts, craters, and scars that greeted me in the mirror every morning.

He ran his hand down my cheek. I flinched, and he moved his fingers away. "Soft, dewy, with a few freckles around your petite nose."

"Petite?" I asked, trying to envision it.

"Yes. Then there are your lips." The way he looked at them made my heart pound. "Your top lip is pointed into two small peaks and is a little thinner than the bottom." He ran his finger over the thin skin, sending shockwaves through my body. "This one is plush and the color of the roses that grow in the gardens." His gaze trickled back to look at me. He leaned in closer. "Your hair is golden, like sand on the beaches. It's woven like silk, falling straight around your shoulders with only a touch of waves between the strands."

My breath hitched. I could have drowned in his words. They rolled off his tongue, melting like chocolate. "Anything else?"

He grinned. "Alas, I am a gentleman, and I will not comment on, um…" He looked at my figure, then shot his eyes back to meet mine.

I laughed. "How considerate."

"I can be much more than considerate." His expression hardened, his words losing their mischievous edge. "For a girl like you, I could be your freedom if you allowed it."

My stomach dipped, and my chest sank. Dizziness fuzzed my thoughts. I was unable to focus on one for more than a second before I lost it.

"Don't think," he whispered. "Please."

He brushed his lips against mine, sending tingles through me. Flickers of touch ran between us. We waited on the edge of anticipation, drowning in each other's eyes. The urge of the kiss took over, and we clashed together. He deepened the kiss, running his hand through my hair. I felt lightheaded. He ran his hand down my back and pulled me against him, tangling us both in a lust all-encompassing. He rested his forehead on mine once we pulled apart. "That was the best kiss," he said, catching his breath, "I've ever had."

I bit my bottom lip, still tasting him. "It's the only kiss I've had."

His eyes shone, more so from the sunlight pouring into the room. "I have searched for the longest time to find someone with whom I could share my heart."

"Wouldn't we get in trouble for this? Sorcerers are not allowed to be with a faery. It is prohibited." Questions tainted my tongue, but I was still lightheaded from the kiss. It dizzied me. I felt like I had drunk several glasses of Abarini.

"I didn't take you for the type of girl who would care."

"I don't."

"Then let's run away together," he begged, tangling his fingers between mine. "Help me free the others and take the sword. As far as I am concerned, I will have fulfilled my promise to the crown, and you would have got revenge for what they did to you. Then we can flee."

I couldn't think straight. It felt like I'd been sucked into a whirlwind with no chance to breathe.

"Come with me," he said pleadingly. "There are so many uninhabited islands we can live on. I know we haven't known each other for long, but the moment I saw you, I knew you were the one for me. There is a light in you, and it lures me like a moth to a flame. You are my flame."

Never had I seen someone bare their heart so openly. His stare burned with a desire that frightened me. I didn't know love or even flirtation before him, and now I had it all. It made me vulnerable, for he was wrong. I was nothing but darkness. I was afraid what would happen if I went with him.

"Are you playing me? Manipulating my heart?" I whispered.

"You don't trust me."

"It's hard for me to trust—"

He squeezed my hands. "Take a chance on us. You *can* trust me. I know all you've had is hurt, but not me. I would never." A small smile tugged his lips. "I never thought I would find love either, yet here you are. We can find peace, together." He seemed so happy. I couldn't bear to say no, and truly everything in me wanted to take him up on his offer. I wanted deeply to believe him and trust him, but there were so many obstacles in the way.

"Love?"

His eyes rounded. "Love."

My breaths quickened. "You are immortal," I stated. "I am not. I will age, and yet time for you will pass slowly."

His eyes widened. "Then let us take the ring from the king. You could live forever with me."

"I don't want to live forever."

He squeezed my hands. "The sword means we can die when we are ready. Don't you see, Evangeline?" His voice went up a whole octave.

"It is as if destiny has laid out everything for us. It was meant to be. I grow surer by the minute."

My master's voice sounded in my mind, jolting me. Pain pinched in my head, screeching through my skull. *"Do not throw away everything for fleeting desire. Tell him no."*

I closed my eyes, forcing him out with every ounce of strength I had. When I opened them again, tears had hazed my vision. "You have been so kind."

His eyebrows drew together. "I don't like the sound of that."

"But I can't leave here."

"It doesn't make sense to me either, but this feels right." He placed his hand on my chest, over where my heart was racing beneath. "Tell me you don't feel what is between us."

My thoughts flickered to the murdered girl, then the necromancer and my father. I had too much baggage. To find love and be happy was a fairytale I could not fall prey to. It didn't happen to girls like me.

"I will help you free the others from the dungeon," I said. "Then disarm my father."

He smiled, dimpling his cheeks. "If that is all you will offer, then I agree, but…" He leaned in, placing his hands on my shoulders. He smelled like rain. It was so evocative. "I must do this." He leaned in again and brushed his lips against mine. "I will not relent in my feelings for you. You are afraid because you have been hidden your whole life, but you deserve joy, and I know you care for me as I do you."

"I do."

"Then give us a chance. We don't get the pleasure of courting first because of who we are, but I promise I will treat you well."

"I believe you will," I said slowly, fumbling my thumbs. I wanted to be happy, to enjoy the moment. I felt my heart weakening to him. "I have not allowed myself a second of joy in my life. Perhaps just a day."

REBECCA L. GARCIA

His expression softened. "Kiss me again."

I squeaked when he grabbed me and pulled me into his arms. "I'm going to show you the world."

My cheeks burned. "I have been so blessed to have you come into my life, now." As the words left my lips, uneasiness settled in me. What if the necromancer hurt him because of me?

"Don't think." He grinned. "I know that face. I've seen it on others when trying to talk themselves out of something."

I placed my hand on his chest. "I'm not."

"So, how will we get the sword from the king?" he questioned.

"Simple." I twirled my fingers, and my magic smoked black, waving up through the air.

His eyes widened. "I'm confused."

"It's a different type of magic, one that cannot be bound by the elements or channeled using relics. It is not one that cannot be used to harm. It is unlimited, and with it, I can bring the guards of the dungeons to their feet. With it, I can force my father's hand and win. I cannot hold off a kingdom, but I can do enough to get you what you need."

He raised his eyebrows. "Beautiful, powerful, humble, *and* kind. How did I deserve this?" He smirked. "Let us get to work then. Let us bring freedom and justice to a corrupt kingdom, if only for a day."

CHAPTER EIGHT

I prepared my good-bye to the long, dark corridors and fading tapestries, my only friends in the place I called home. "I will not miss it here," I muttered under my breath. That was when I felt the pain in my stomach. He was fighting his way back in. As he did, a hand tugged my arm and pulled me into a corner.

"I will make you suffer." My youngest sister, Primrose, glared at me. "I will lock you away, in unending torment." She grabbed a fistful of my hair. "You will get no peace from death."

"Don't screech." I pushed Primrose away with a gentle nudge. She was so petite. She'd always been the smallest of us all. "The spell will lift."

"Zalia told me of your hexes and evil. How you wish wickedness upon us. I do not trust to live my life knowing a sister meaning me harm lies in the shadows, waiting to find a way to ruin my happiness."

I grabbed her wrist and tugged her toward me. "If you come at me again, I will hurt you, for real this time. You, my other siblings, Father," I spat, "have brought me nothing but misery, and you're here threatening my life." I let go of her. "Stupid girl."

"Father says you are darkness," she said, rubbing her wrist.

I clenched my jaw. "Then you better not get too close."

She shifted from foot to foot, uncertainty lacing her features. "The baron is coming to court tomorrow eve. Make sure they're gone by then." She pointed at her spots.

"What of mine? Hmm? Yours will fade and yet I am stuck with them."

Confusions swept her soft features.

"Leave," I ordered before she could argue further. "Now."

I attempted to leave the passageway, but Zalia strutted toward us. I looked up at the ceiling. "God give me strength," I said under my breath. "What is it? Have you come to scream at me also?"

"I know you have been with Caspian."

My heart hammered. "That's preposterous."

Primrose glowered, hiding behind Zalia. "She threatened me."

I rolled my eyes. "Enough from you." I snapped my fingers, and her mouth sewed shut.

Zalia scowled, looking from me to Primrose who was screaming behind closed lips. "What did you do to her?"

"She always did talk too much. The spell will lift once I walk away."

Her eyes flashed red. "Why have you requested an audience with Father? You've avoided him all these years. Why now?"

I sensed fear in her tone. "He has accepted, hasn't he?"

"He is less tolerant than me."

My lips curved into an unsettling smile. "Good." I lifted my skirts and pushed past her. Before I reached the corner, I stopped and looked back. "I never wanted to hurt you, you know. Despite what you may believe, I never killed Charleston. I know you cannot always control your powers. You gave in to delusions, and I worry you still do. Be careful, Zalia, for I won't always be here to protect you, and the next time you let your magic overtake you, Father will have your head."

"I would never…" She spluttered, but hesitance caught her last words.

"You know I speak truth. I hid the pain from you, taking it myself, but no more. Not today." I looked my sisters up and down before turning the corner. I'd never been close to Primrose or Selena, but I had been once to Zalia.

I couldn't look back. Instead, I pushed forward, forcing one foot in front of the other. Nervousness buzzed on my lips, or perhaps it was the kiss from Caspian that lingered.

I was certain I was falling in love. I couldn't explain the feeling in me; although things were moving fast, he was all I saw when I looked to the future. A hope… a chance for happiness. He was everything I wanted in a man, a love requited.

***

I shivered as I walked up to the king's office. Pulling the hood of my cloak over my head, I hurried past two guards. The flames from the torches on the wall danced, their shadows rippled.

I held my breath.

"I swear these passages are haunted." The guard let out a shaky breath. "The princess is coming for an audience with the king. Have you seen her?"

"No," the other said.

Avoiding them both, I turned the corner and took the long way around. Their voices faded, their conversation unintelligible. My heels clicked against the ancient stone. I blinked twice, then the voice thundered into my mind.

"DO NOT SHUT ME OUT."

I pressed my hands against my temples, squeezing him out. "Get out!" I begged. "Leave me."

"DO NOT DEFY ME."

I focused on my kiss with Caspian and was consumed by fluttering in my stomach. After a few moments, he fizzled away, leaving my head clear. I needed that if I was going to best my father, a man known to rule with an iron fist and always chose head over heart.

I reached the double doors and emerged from blackness. The guards looked me up and down, along with four nobles and three highborn girls. A servant stared from behind them, unnoticed by the rest, carrying a tray.

"Princess Evangeline," a guard announced. A man sounded a trumpet, and the other guard opened the door. I'd never been announced before. I hated all the eyes on me. I was uncertain why the king was allowing such a public meeting. He'd hidden me away for so long, I had forgotten what the main rooms in the castle looked like.

I spotted a noble and his son. I rolled my eyes at his court-trained, charming smile. They'd stoop to any lengths for favor, even smiling at an ugly princess.

Those around me, their scandalous, wanting eyes regarding me, saved me embarrassment. Not one looked disgusted. Father must have warned them not to, a kindness that put guilt in my conscience.

Cautiously, I walked into the large office, which was a crescent shape. A desk ran along the far wall, polished and covered with ornate boxes, a cigar tray, parchment, ink, quills, and other trinkets. The man behind it stared at me with eyes of steel, his expression hardened. His youthful curls had flattened a little under the weight of his crown. I flitted my stare down to the Ring of

Immortalem. The object delayed his death, until he relinquished its power willingly.

"Daughter."

"No need for niceties."

His eyes rounded. "You dare talk to me with such brashness?"

"Yes." I twirled my fingers, and black magic fizzled midair.

His thin lips downturned. "What did you do?"

"You will release the fae in the dungeons to my care and hand over the Sword of Impervius. If you do not comply, I will rain down a hell on this castle unlike any you have ever seen. You will suffer, your heirs will scream, and your people will lose everything."

He laughed mockingly. "I do not bow to my lesser."

"I feared you for so long, and I see now I was wrong to do so. I have more power than you, and with it, I will take everything from you as you took from me. Tell me the truth. Did you place this curse on me?"

His eyes narrowed, his lip twitching at the corner. "Yes." His nostrils flared. "You had something evil in you. My seer saw visions of murder and blood in your future. The only way to stop it was to place the curse of the beast on you. I did it to save my other children, but your mother hated me for it before she died." He picked up a paperweight and weighed it in his hand. "Nevertheless, you killed Charleston."

Tears pricked my eyes. "I never hurt him. I stopped Zalia."

"What fairytales you tell yourself." He slammed the paperweight onto his desk, cracking the wood. "You do not remember, but something lives inside you, and it destroys anything good." The words were hissed through his teeth. Cold shivered down my spine.

"I wouldn't—"

Caspian emerged from the shadows. I'd sent him to a passageway linking him to this room. The conversations I'd overheard behind the walls were priceless.

"Don't listen to him," Caspian said. "He is lying."

"What is this?" the king spat, disheveling his crown. "You bring a fae to me?"

"You brought him here."

Caspian stepped forward. "I know everything. The faeries in the dungeon... how you torture them! The king will know of this."

"Yes, and I will be the one to end you." I smiled, ear to ear. "I have great magic now, Father. Deadly, some say. I made a deal."

Fear laced his stare. "Tell me you didn't make a deal with the necromancer."

I swallowed hard. "Yes... I... How do you know about him?"

"He is the one who cursed you, child." He growled softly. "I presume that's how he's managed to infiltrate you, through it."

"What?"

"He made a deal with me, for the ring." It glinted on his finger. "They belonged to him. I didn't want to tell you the truth, but as he is in control if you, you should know how dangerous he is. Because of him, your mother is dead!"

"You cursed me so you could live forever?" I growled, my stare growing murderous. "Then how fitting that you shall join my mother at his hand too."

"Guards!" my father shouted. The doors flew open, and they rushed inside. I tried to stop them, but my magic wasn't working. My lips parted. Caspian waited for me to do something, but I couldn't.

"My magic." I gasped. The necromancer had cut me off. "No. No." I looked at the palm of my hands, wild-eyed. "Give it back. He will kill me, us."

The sound of clashing and hollowed screams brought me to my knees. My father's voice sliced through me. "You shouldn't have told him." He glared at me. "How will I explain this to the fae king?"

My mind faltered when I locked eyes with Caspian. Blood gushed out of Caspian's chest, pulsating with each beat of his heart. I reached out to touch him as the scarlet dripped down his clothing, but he faded, then turned to ash as Father wrenched the sword back.

"No." I choked. "No, Caspian." I reached around the ground, touching what remained of him. My tears fell onto the stone. "NO!"

They grabbed my arms, then my legs. "Take her to the dungeons and prepare the executioner's block."

CHAPTER NINE

Scraping my bare feet against grainy sand mixed with dirt, I shuffled back and pushed myself against the wall. Sunlight arrowed through the bars of my window. I choked on my tears, coughing until I'd fallen onto all fours. "Caspian, I'm sorry," I said aloud, although he couldn't hear me.

"You!" I growled at the necromancer, begging him to hear me. "You took my mother. Cursed me. Lied to me."

"You needed me."

I sat upright, digging my fingers into my legs. "So you finally answer." The corner of my lip twitched. "You said you were gaining power, to find your lost love." I felt vulnerability in him, if only for a moment. "What does it have to do with me?" I looked up at the light. He was too quiet. "Unless, was she of my bloodline. Why did you target me? I didn't come to you like the others looking for power. You came to me, forcing a curse on me, then using that curse to get close to me. Why?"

His silence was deafening. I picked up a jagged rock and placed it against my wrist. "If I am nothing to you, then you will not mind if I die. I have nothing to live for anyway."

"Don't do it. Put it down, and I will tell you everything."

I scoffed. "Your threats were empty. You need me alive."

"Your father came to me. Many have, looking for power, for immortality, or to bring their loved ones back from the dead. He wanted to live forever, but he knew the cost was out of my control. For a life extended, one must die. I didn't know it would be the queen, and he was

distraught, but she was never my cost. It was a favor."

My eye twitched. I could hear the tortured screams of the fae next door. "Yes, my curse."

"It was the only way I could get inside your head. I latched myself to your magic, and the loneliness turned you to me. It was in my agreement with your father."

"I will die before I let you use me again."

"Before you do something you might regret, you must know that your curse... It is only you who sees yourself as the beast. No one else does. It is an old magic, one used on the vain, but for you, it made you isolated, and I needed you that way. Understand."

I raised my eyebrows. "If that's all—"

"It's not. I can bring Caspian back from the dead."

"What lies you tell. You have done nothing but bring darkness to this world, and Caspian wouldn't have wanted that. Your doing anything for me puts me in your debt."

"See reason. I will grant you a large pocket of power, enough to raise Caspian, untethered to me."

"What do you want in return?" I spat.

"You are part of the ritual to bring her back. My wife. She died during the plague a long time ago."

"How can I bring her back?"

"There is a headstone, with her blood on it. I will tell you where to find it. You can use it, use my power, to perform a ritual."

"No." I scowled. "You would have brought her back yourself or used one of my ancestors to do it."

"It had to be the firstborn woman in her direct bloodline, and you are the first female born since who is a direct descendant. However, you must sacrifice twelve people to do it."

"That's why you made me kill the servant girl. You were readying me, grooming me to kill more."

"I will do anything for the woman I love."

"What of you once it is done? With your great power, will you bring more torment?"

"I wish only to have her."

I didn't trust him, but I did my best to keep my thoughts quiet. "Untether yourself from me, grant me the power, and I will do it."

"Why would I be so foolish?"

"Because if you do not, then I will kill myself."

Silence hung between us. I tried to block out the screams, but they grew louder.

"I will grant you enough power to perform the ritual and bring your lover back to life. Once you have completed it, you will be free. Is it a deal?"

"Yes."

I warmed with magic. It tingled through my fingers and up my arms. As it did, he left. For the first time in over a decade, I felt weightless. I hadn't realized what heaviness I had carried around with him inside me.

The necromancer was right, however. He was foolish.

Using my new powers, I aimed a shock of bright light at the lock, and the door swung open. "Don't," I warned the men rushing toward me.

They hesitated but paused for only a second before pursuing. I snapped my fingers, willing slumber and darkness from the dungeons, and within it they fell. I opened my eyes and looked around at the locked doors.

One by one, they clicked open. The magic I held was immense and filled me. I was brimming, boiling over. The fae slumped out the doors, looking pale. Some didn't leave their cells despite no longer being locked in. I knew I needed to help them, for Caspian.

Gathering one in my arms, I helped him to his feet. I'd get them out of the castle through the secret passageways, then I'd kill my father.

***

His face was sullen under the pale light. I tilted my head to meet his cold stare. "You would attempt to kill me, but you will die first."

I curled my hands into fists, reigning shaky breaths to an appearance of calmness. "I am not afraid to die." I curled my lips in behind my teeth and bit down. "I do not fear the unknown, like you. I am not weak."

He snarled, his lip twitching at the corner. "You don't scare me, Evangeline." My name spat from his wicked tongue like venom. "Your mother loved you, no matter how you looked or acted, and I am grateful she died before she could see what you became." He paused, and his breaths rattled as he glared. "I locked you away because you are darkness." He elongated each word. They sent shivers down my spine. "You enjoyed misery, so I left you in its company. The necromancer was right to choose you to curse. He needed you, begged me for you because he sensed your wickedness."

"No! He chose me because I am the first girl in the direct bloodline." I took a step forward, balling my fists while tears crept down my cheeks. "As for my darkness, it was because you left me isolated. I was miserable, for you showed my sisters and brothers love and never me. Then you took the only person who showed me love." I closed my eyes. Caspian's blue eyes weaved through my memories, bringing a smile to my tear-stained lips. "I don't fear death because I know that when I walk into the afterlife, I will be joined by Caspian. It's easy to welcome the end, knowing I will see the one I love again." I opened my eyes to see Father's graying face. "You do not love. You only want power, using the people who adored you. No one will be waiting for you in the abyss. The necromancer will be enraged, but I will not be alive to face his wrath." I was growing weaker by the minute. "I could have brought back Caspian, then I realized you'd still rule, and it would be a dishonor to Caspian's memory. You have the ring, and unless you relinquish it willingly, you cannot die."

His eyes flitted around the room, uncertainty in his expression. "Bring back the fae instead. I'll let you go and live out your days with him. Don't make me kill you by your failed assassination."

"Mercy." I scoffed. "I doubt it. You sense it, don't you?"

The heaviness from my powers weighed on us both. "What did you do?" he asked.

"It took every ounce of power I had to do it."

He slammed his fist on the desk. "Don't mess with nations."

"It's almost done," I said, feeling my life draining. It had taken too much from me to curse the Objects of Kai. Such ancient, strong relics…

My fingernails were caked with dried blood and mud from where I'd led the broken fae out of the castle and into a field. I grabbed the Sword of Impervius and held it in my trembling hands. It burned my skin, sizzling loudly.

"You see, Father. They're cursed, just like I was."

His eyes widened. Without a thought, he pulled off the ring, worried it'd burn him like the sword did me, but it wouldn't; my plan worked.

I tilted my head upward to watch as life left his pale-gray eyes. He was older in his final moments, fragile without the gold crown on top of his head. His conker-brown waves turned silver, then white. My lips curled up when he took his final breath. He was the last one I needed to kill. No more blood would be on my hands, and now I had to die.

I closed my eyes when Zalia entered the room. "Don't wear the ring," I said through shallow breaths.

She dropped to my side, holding my hand. "I listened to everything through the door." She croaked. "I'm so sorry." Her tears fell, thick and fast. "I'm afraid. You were right. My magic is untamed. I can't rule."

"Be kind to the fae. Unite our kingdoms," I whispered as I took my final breaths. I could see Caspian now, waiting for me. There was no more death, no pain, only peace.

The End

Thank you for reading *Ruin*, a prequel to *The Fate of Crowns*, releasing January 5th, 2021.

Ruin is the origin story of the curses of the Objects of Kai and of Evangeline and her lover, Caspian. In The Fate of Crowns, Evangeline's story is briefly mentioned as it is centuries later, and I felt compelled to bring light to why she cursed the Objects of Kai, how her curse came to be, and why Berovia is the only kingdom where fae and sorcerers live peacefully side by side.

For a sneak peek at the first chapter of The Fate of Crowns, *book one, read on below.*

SNEAK PEEK AT
THE FATE OF CROWNS

RELEASING JANUARY 5TH, 2021

1

The sunrise glistened in a thousand shades of oranges and reds behind rolling clouds of silver. I shifted my eyes down to the castle grounds. Neat beds of blue and purple flowers lined the path. Roses entwined metal arches, leading down stone steps to the left. In the center was a tall, stone fountain. Orange hues bounced off the frozen water at the bottom.

Magic pulsated through my staff, beating like an open heart. I flexed my fingers, then turned away from the window to take in Morgana. Tall and willowy, she stood stronger than the other women at court. She leaned over a teapot that leaked droplets as she turned off the stovetop. She then attempted to untangle a puff of brown hair. Her orb-like eyes regarded me as I took a seat next to the slanted shelves. Melted candles and mismatched books sat on it, collecting dust. Light poured into the room, illuminating the wisps of dust in the air. I flicked back my black waves, then chewed on my nails.

"Try this time," she said encouragingly.

I repressed the urge to roll my eyes. She treated more like an apprentice most days than the princess I was. Although, she was my only friend in the castle.

Something clonked from inside her deep pockets as she walked toward me. Thrusting a china cup into my hands, she cast her eyes downward. The leaves had gathered into the shape of a sword. Her expectant stare bored into me as I breathed in the evocative smell of heather and lavender. Morgana waited for my insight, but I didn't have the *gift* that she insisted I had. I waited for her to tire of standing by, for me to get a vision, and call on it herself. I needed to know what it meant, but only Morgana could foresee.

I looked sideways as quickened breaths and hollow footsteps grew close. A sorceress had come for a reading. The girl's eyebrows were set downward as she hovered in the doorway. She cleared her throat, drawing Morgana's attention.

"I need a reading."

Morgana glanced at me as I pressed my nails into the flesh of my palms. The familiar flicker of anger crossed my expression.

"I'm in a session," Morgana replied.

"Don't you know who I am?" The girl tapped her fingers rhythmically against her side. I could tell she was anxious, although she tried to hide it. I guessed from the new string of pearls around her neck that she was new, to be one of my mother's ladies. Her skin was still tanned. She had come from the south, where there was still sunshine in the summer months. She wore heavy earrings, although they left red marks on her lobes. She wasn't used to wearing fancy things.

"Come back later," I ordered, my patience wearing thin.

Her lips pinched together. She opened her mouth to argue but paused when her eyes met mine. They were almond brown and filled with indecision.

"Your Highness." Her words trembled. She sank into a deep bow. Her silky hair reflected the sunlight, her dark-brown strands glistening out from the black as it spilled around her face. She chewed on her bottom lip as she rose upward.

"Come... back... later." I teetered on the edge of rage. The teacup was still warm in my hand; I had half a mind to throw it at her.

Morgana's eyes flicked to mine, warning in her stare. She blew out a tense breath, then turned toward the girl. "Please, come back later in the morning."

The girl's lips barely moved as she muttered an apology. She turned and hurried down the spiraling steps. Her heels clicked as they hit ancient stone.

"I'll have her sent away!" I threatened and squeezed the china tightly. "Who even wakes up this early?"

Morgana circled my chair. "You must not let your anger get the better of you, Winter."

"But she—"

"You know better." Her tangled eyebrow hooked upward.

"I guess we won't know what it means now." I clenched my jaw. The girl had disrupted the flow of energy. I leaned my staff against the chair, then looked over at the bundles of flowers. They had been wrapped individually and piled on one of the shelves at the back of the room. Morgana sold them to get more gold coins. Her collections were expensive, things that were hard to get ahold of in Magaelor.

She paused in front of me and searched my gaze as she had done many times before. "Your soul drowns in the river of your rage. You will lose yourself if you do not learn to control it."

I wanted to swallow the fury from my expression, but it lingered around my frown, a tell Morgana always picked up on.

"It won't work unless you're calm," she stated.

Her eyes closed, and she wrapped her fingers around mine. She searched through the clutter in my mind. Slowly, she untangled my web of thoughts.

It felt like fire at first—a flame that licked through the veins in my arms and to my chest. I wanted to pull away, but the teacup, still in our grasp, grounded me. I needed to know my future. I was a cardboard princess, an empty crown. Pointless. The truth tugged at my heart. My father had never paid much attention to me until today. He looked at me as if he were seeing me for the first time since I was a young child. I was a woman now—sixteen and ready for a purpose. Perhaps I would finally be useful to him. I was never going to take the throne. That was my brother's fate, but I needed one too. I was desperate, and Morgana knew it. She kept me waiting, testing my patience. She did it on purpose, to teach me restraint. It irritated me into shaking my leg, but I knew better than to go against her. She could out-stubborn us all.

Sparks flickered under her touch and through my skin. The flame sensation turned to ice, freezing me from the inside. Finally, a wave of serenity washed through me as destiny revealed a message. I couldn't make it out—Morgana had pulled it from my head before I could—but I sensed something else. A kiss lingered on my lips, but from whom, and what did it have to do with my fate?

Morgana let go, my fingers quivered, and the teacup tumbled from my grip. She stepped back when the china shattered over the uneven ground. Her hands were charred black.

"What happened?"

She exhaled a raspy breath. "Death. I saw death."

My breath hitched. Broken shards pointed upward at me, and the tea leaves clung to them. Her watery eyes locked onto mine.

"Whose?" I asked, afraid of the answer.

She fished into her deep pocket and pulled out three smooth, gray stones. She flipped them over to reveal their symbols. Running her fingertip along the ridges, she closed her eyes. She shivered, snaking her back up as she did.

"The deaths will mark the beginning."

I stood, leveling myself with her. "Deaths?" I questioned, noticing the plural. "Of whom? Morgana, what did you see?" I pled.

"I'm not sure. A boy, I do not recognize him, then another... in a battle." Her eyes opened again. The brown in them had turned to the color of smoke. "A crown. I see a crown."

Hairs stood erect on my arms. "What one?"

"The only one that matters."

***

I walked somberly to the banquet hall, weaving through ancient passageways and long corridors. My confusion from the reading flitted through my mind like flies. I reached the open doors. Tables lined both sides of the grand room. I took my seat at the back, away from prying eyes. Shuttered light beamed through the arched windows, making the chandeliers glimmer. Everything about Ash Court shone. The stones on the walls were embedded with millions of tiny crystals. It was enchanting, especially to the visitors. Disguised as my home was actually a fortress against those who wanted us dead. It also served as a place for dignitaries to stay, rooms solely to entertain. Me and my family were the main event, the real-life royals people begged to see. We had to pose for pictures and smile at strangers. I tried my hardest to stay out of the limelight, which was easy when standing next to my brother, André.

I squinted at the window. Fractures of blue light bounced off the diamonds set in my tiara, drawing attention to where I sat. I hated wearing the heavy thing, but Mother insisted. I never did desire to attract those only a crown could entice. I grimaced and held my staff close to my chest. I watched the beady, wanting eyes of noblemen from the tables in front of mine as they stared up at my head. Making it a point to look away from them, I clutched the ash wood until my knuckles turned white. Beating magic pulsated up through the polished wood and into my hands. One spell and I could turn them all into the slimy eels they truly were, but I couldn't cast one without bringing attention to my afterhours reading materials and Morgana's illicit collection. Using banned spells was punishable by death. Although as a princess, I was sure I could forgo execution, but she would not.

"Stop it." A girl giggled, then nudged the side of a young man whose eyes were alight with lust. They passed by me, dipped their heads when they saw me, then hurried out the door.

I knew that look all too well. I'd only exchanged it with one other.

I glanced around the banquet hall, which was painted in silks of silver and blue to signify the fae's visit to the castle. I preferred those colors when compared to the awful pinks and lilacs that had been forced upon me since the wedding. Since *she* had come into our life. Florence Montague, now formally known as the Princess of Magaelor. She was closer to the throne than I was since marrying my brother, and she never wasted an opportunity to remind me of it.

I watched from the back of the room as she and her ladies-in-waiting began the waltz. I didn't bother forcing a smile or clapping. Instead, I silently judged them from the security of the shadows. The ladies' heels tapped against the polished marble. People sat at long, oak tables which were crammed with platters and plates of jam and lemon tarts, pink crystals from the lake which made any drink taste sweet, and roasted dragons' eggs, a delicacy.

My mother peered at me from the top table as I reached for a tart. She wore the same disapproving look she greeted me with every day. I retracted, then picked up my cup of peppermint tea and sipped. She didn't like me eating too many jam tarts. *"It's not good for a princess to be stuffing their face in public,"* she would say, chastising me whenever she spotted me eating sugary treats. She hardly ever ate; you could tell from the sullen skin hanging from her cheekbones and her pale, chalky appearance. Her hooded eyes were bloodshot as she stared out over those enjoying their breakfast.

The dance finished and everyone applauded. I spotted the girl from the tower room who had interrupted my reading and shot her a scathing look, but it was wasted. She was too busy eyeing a nobleman's son. I wrestled with the idea of having her sent home. Although, I had been wrong about one thing; she wasn't one of my mother's ladies. She was Florence's. More had come. How many did she need? I had an entourage of zero, except for the maids who attended my needs.

Ruffles covered their dresses. She only picked women who she'd deemed uglier than her, but the new girl was pretty, and Florence looked displeased. She was vain, and no one could outshine her. They never did, except for when the fae visited court. A smirk tugged at my lips. I loved watching Florence squirm. My hatred of her far overpowered my irritation of the girl who made her jealous.

Florence turned her head, and her ash-blonde waves danced around her shoulders as she did. She searched the room, looking for Andre, who hadn't paid her the slightest bit of attention since I had joined the festivities. At what I presumed was an attempt to get his attention, she drank her liquor and proceeded to flirt with any man in her vicinity. A shrill, high-pitched laugh resonated through the room as she fell back on some poor guy's lap.

I sighed loudly enough to catch the attention of a woman in front of me who looked at me with shrouded annoyance. I hadn't done much to mask my dislike for Florence. Neither did my mother, who felt the same, but the others in the castle loved her. I didn't like Florence for many reasons, but arguably, her worst trait was her indiscretion. She acted however she pleased while wearing the Mortis family name. She argued with Andre in public and was more impulsive than even the likes of my brother. I only hoped he would rid us of her soon.

No one had expected him to marry so quickly. He had always enjoyed life as a bachelor, but I supposed it had to happen sometime or another. Marrying her was his way of getting it over and done with, obeying my parents' wishes while cementing his future rule with a simple *I do*. After all, he was the crown prince, and future kings needed a queen. I just wished he'd picked anyone but her.

"Don't get upset," Morgana said as she took the empty seat next to mine. "You'll end up with frown lines."

I narrowed my eyes at her. "You never come down for breakfast. Why are you here?"

She lowered her voice to a whisper. "Your father encouraged me to do so. He has an important announcement."

I rolled my eyes. "We all know what encouraged means."

"Yes, but while he is in power, we must do as he says."

"For now," I said and looked at my brother. I couldn't wait until he would take the throne. He would be the best king this kingdom had ever seen. Aside from his taste in women, he was the perfect ruler—fair, with strong and traditional values, and an innate ability to broker negotiations like no other.

I balled my fist when Florence grabbed the attention of the room by laughing too loudly again.

It was only two weeks ago when everything had changed and she was inevitably pushed into our lives.

It was a rare, sunny afternoon when I'd snuck into the council hall to listen to the trade deals my father and his council were trying to make with the dark fae. Hiding behind a wood panel at the top of a secret passageway, I had listened as the council's voices rose in an uproar. They were attempting to obtain more mugroot, which grew native to the Snowy Peaks in the fae's half of the kingdom. My father argued the price was twice what it should be and that they were exploiting them due to their dislike for sorcerers. Jasper and Amara, the ambassadors from the dark fae court, argued back. Accusations were thrown from both sides. I watched through a small crack in the wood when the doors burst open. Andre sauntered in with a twenty-something blonde in tow, who I'd later be introduced to as my future sister-in-law. They had met at the Academy of Sorcery, and he told everyone how she was his greatest love. I groaned. It wouldn't last. It never did. Florence bounced behind him, all smiles and pearly white teeth, her eyes filled with hope. It wasn't the first time he had brought a girl back to the castle, but it was the first time he had talked about marriage. Andre was easily distracted by beautiful things, and it was only a matter of time until the next pretty girl came along with a smart mouth and Florence would be forgotten. At least, I had thought. Despite our objections, the wedding came fast. They were married within a week. I supposed it was a good thing for her. At least she had got a crown before his attention drifted elsewhere.

A hearty chuckle from a man near my table pulled my attention to the festivities. I'd missed that morning's council meeting—and the one from yesterday—after spending my mornings in Morgana's tower room. I only hoped I hadn't missed anything of interest.

"What are you thinking about?" Morgana asked. She looked so out of place among the fashionably dressed ladies and suited men. Her loose-fitting purple dress was patterned with daisies.

"Just remembering when I met Florence."

"She will never be queen," Morgana whispered. "As the future currently is. It's all I have seen. She ends up engaged to another."

My lips curled upward. "At least today has had *some* good news then."

"News you will keep to yourself."

I looked at my brother again. He was charming Amara, who had come back to visit the court to talk about another trade deal. She twirled around, her bright-blue skirt billowing outward. Her black, flowing hair shone with scattered contrasting strands of white. Her high cheekbones and round, dark eyes made her irresistible to all around her, which was probably why the dark fae king, Azrael, had sent her along with Jasper to solidify deals. After all, who could resist the beauty of a faery?

Morgana stood. "I'm going to get a drink. Would you like anything?"

I shook my head and watched her walk away. When she reached the drinks table, I caught a menacing grin from Jasper. He was standing next to the string quartet.

My heart raced.

I averted my eyes from his penetrating stare. He was my brother's best friend, which was unusual as fae and sorcerers seldom mixed outside of discussing deals. Nonetheless, he and Andre were like two peas in a pod. They were both charming, charismatic, and had a way of magnetizing the people around them. They could pull on the unseen strings of everyone at court. I wasn't ignorant to the power Andre held over the castle, including my parents. It was why I always stayed in his good graces. If I couldn't get something I wanted, I could count on him to get it for me.

I looked over at the table again. Jasper was still looking at me. My face reddened.

Glasses clinked, silencing the room. I turned my attention to the two tall thrones. My father was smiling but not his usual public smile, where there was a slight curve to his lips with no crease below the eyes. No, this one was genuine. His eyes shined as the curves rounded up, balling his cheeks. The light from the chandelier waved through the silver hues of hair beneath his crown set with rubies and emeralds. His deep voice rumbled. "Gathered dignitaries, friends, and"—he lifted his glass to the direction I was standing— "family. I am delighted to announce a new, strong relationship today between fae and sorcerers. Unity between us for the first time in seven hundred years."

His words pulsated through the room; no one had expected them. A buzz of anxiety hung over us. How had he managed the impossible?

His voice grew louder with each beat, booming out from the absolute silence. "Our alliance has become possible through the betrothal of my daughter, Winter Mortis, and the crown fae prince, Blaise Lazarus."

Heads turned in my direction. Chatter rose, and unintelligible whispers surrounded me. Exhaling a shaky breath, I closed my eyes. My father's discerning gaze was focused on me when I opened them again. He was waiting for my reaction, and in front of everyone who mattered to him, I knew what I needed to do. I forced a small smile.

He turned his attention back to the room. His voice faded out. My ears rang loudly as shock rooted me to the spot. Jasper looked at me from the other side of the hall. He had to have known, which must've been why they were visiting. *I* was the trade deal.

Y A F A N T A S Y

REBECCA L. GARCIA

Rebecca lives in San Antonio, Texas, with her husband and son. Born and raised in England, she can be found at her desk drinking tea, writing new worlds, and designing.

Rebecca devoured every book she was given from the age of five and fell in love with magical worlds. When she got older, her imagination grew with her, and she delved into writing strong characters and vast worlds.

When she's not writing or spending time with her family, you can find her traveling and hosting book signings with Spellbinding Events.

The Fate of Crowns, book one, releases January 5th, 2021 with the following four books releasing between February and May.

Follow Rebecca here:

Facebook:

facebook.com/rebeccalgarciabooks

Instagram:

instagram.com/rebeccalgarciabooks

Join her reader group for updates and discussions:

facebook.com/groups/rebeccasbeauties

Twitter:

twitter.com/rlgarciabooks

Website:

rebeccalgarciabooks.com

Newsletter:

bit.ly/NewsletterRebeccaLGarcia